share your love from
the very start!

D1301307

Copyright © 2020 by Sandra Magsamen
Cover and internal design © 2020 by Sourcebooks
Text and illustrations © 2020 by Hanny Girl Productions, Inc. sandramagsamen.com

Sourcebooks and the colophon are registered trademarks of Sourcebooks

All rights reserved.

Published by Sourcebooks Wonderland, an imprint of Sourcebooks Kids
P.O. Box 4410, Naperville, Illinois 60567-4410
(630) 961-3900
sourcebookskids.com

Library of Congress Cataloging-in-Publication Data is on file with the publisher.

Source of Production: Shenzhen Wing King Tong Paper Products, Shenzhen, Guangdong Province, China
Date of Production: December 2019
Run Number: 5016823

Printed and bound in China.
WKT 10 9 8 7 6 5 4 3 2 1

Marysville Public Library
231 S. Plum Street
Marysville, OH 43040
937-642-1876

DISCARD

wishes
for
little one

(a heartfelt gift filled with special wishes for baby)

by Sandra Magsamen

sourcebooks
wonderland

We've gathered to shower you with love my dear...

and We made
a book of
wishes
for you
to hear!

We are your family, your friends and your neighbors too...

we are so excited to welcome you!

We're **thrilled** that you are on your **way...**

and we look forward to **watching** you **grow** each day!

Our hearts are filled with hopes, dreams and lots of joy too...

our wishes are
a gift to
inspire you
your whole
life through!

You see, you're our newest shining star...

we'll always love you for who YOU are!

So, as you read these **wishes** written just for **you**, please remember that **wishes** really do come **true!**

write a wish
from your **heart.**

share your **love** from the very **start!**

write a wish
from your heart.